We're Going on a Pumpkin Hunt

by Steve Metzger

Illustrated by Mike Byrne

Scholastic Inc.

ISBN 978-1-338-33022-9

10 9 8 7 6 5 4 3 2   19 20 21 22 23
Printed in U. S. A.   40
First printing 2019

Book design by Jennifer Rinaldi

We're going on a pumpkin hunt.
We'll find them on the ground.
We're hoping they're bright orange
and big and wide and round!

We're coming to a hay bale—
a huge and prickly hay bale.

We can't go through it.
What are we going to do?

Climb, climb, climb
to the other side.

No pumpkins here—but we won't stop looking!

We're going on a pumpkin hunt.
We'll find them on the ground.

We're hoping they're bright orange
and big and wide and round!

We're coming to a maze—
a winding maze of corn.

We can't go around it.
What are we going to do?

March, march, march
to the other side.

No pumpkins here–
but we won't stop looking!

We're going on a pumpkin hunt.
We'll find them on the ground.

We're hoping they're bright orange
and big and wide and round!

We're coming to a barnyard—
a loud and muddy barnyard.

We can't walk across it.
What are we going to do?

Ride, ride, ride
to the other side.

No pumpkins here–but we won't stop looking!

We're going on a pumpkin hunt.
We'll find them on the ground.

We're hoping they're bright orange and big and wide and round!

We're coming to a pond—
a wide and sparkling pond.

We can't jump over it.
What are we going to do?

Paddle, paddle, paddle
to the other side.

Wait a minute!
Vines and leaves are growing on the ground!
And look! There's something else!
It's big . . . it's round . . . it's orange.
It's a . . .

PUMPKIN!!!
Oh my! There are lots of them!

Big ones!
Small ones!
Round ones!

Skinny ones!
Smooth ones!
Bumpy ones!

We did it!

Uh-oh. It's getting dark.
Ka-boom! What's that noise?
It's THUNDER!

Let's go!

Paddle the canoe!
Paddle, paddle, paddle.

Ride the horses!
Ride, ride, ride.

March through the maze!
March, march, march.

Climb over the haystack!
Climb, climb, climb.

We're home!

We went on a pumpkin hunt.
We found them on the ground.
That thunder really scared us,
but now we're safe and sound.

Math and Cooking Fun with Pumpkin Seeds!

Try this engaging and educational activity in the classroom . . . or at home!

You will need:
- 1 medium-size pumpkin
- 2 teaspoons olive oil
- pinch of sea salt
- pumpkin-carving tool
- large spoon
- strainer or colander
- kitchen towel
- bowl
- sheet of parchment paper
- baking sheet

Helpful hint:
Since this is a messy project, you might want to cover your table with a plastic tablecloth. Aprons or smocks are also recommended.

Pre-cooking directions:

1. Before you begin
Carve out the top part of the pumpkin (around the stem) and replace it before the children join you.

2. Display your pumpkin
Encourage vocabulary by asking children to describe what it looks like. Pass the pumpkin around and ask for words that describe its texture.

3. Make estimates
Ask children to guess how many pumpkin seeds are inside your pumpkin. Record their estimates. (If you have a tape measure, you can also record their estimates about the pumpkin's circumference. Then measure it.)

4. Scoop out the insides
After you remove the stem, ask children to take turns scooping out the pulp and seeds. (This would also be a good time to elicit descriptive language about its texture.)

5. Separate the seeds from the pulp
Encourage children to make two piles: pulp and seeds. (During this activity, you might want to ask children if they'd like to revise their pumpkin seed estimates.)

6. Clean the seeds
Continue separating the pulp from the seeds by thoroughly rinsing them in a colander.

7. Dry the seeds
Take turns patting the seeds dry with a kitchen cloth or paper towels. (Note: the seeds might stick more to paper towels.)

8. Count your seeds
Once all the seeds are dry, ask children to count them — one by one. (It might be easier to make groups of ten.) Compare the total number of counted seeds to their estimates.

Cooking directions:

Note: To ensure a safe and accident-free activity, only adults should take part in oven-related directions.
Also, check that pumpkin seeds have sufficiently cooled off before children touch and taste.

1. Preheat your oven to 350° F.
2. Line a baking sheet with parchment paper.
3. Toss the pumpkin seeds with the olive oil and sea salt in your bowl.
4. Transfer a single layer of pumpkin seeds to the baking sheet.
5. Bake for approximately 30 minutes, or until the seeds are deeply golden.
6. Remove the seeds from the oven and allow them to cool.
7. Enjoy a delicious snack! (Ask children to describe how their toasted pumpkin seeds taste.)